Wedding Bell Blues

Book 8

Wedding Bell Blues

JILL SANTOPOLO

Aladdin

NEW YORK LONDON TORONTO SYDNEY NEW DELHI

🪔 ALADDIN

An imprint of Simon & Schuster Children's Publishing Division
1230 Avenue of the Americas, New York, NY 10020
This Aladdin hardcover edition February 2016
Text copyright © 2016 by Simon & Schuster, Inc.
Jacket illustrations copyright © 2016 by Cathi Mingus
Also available in an Aladdin paperback edition.
All rights reserved, including the right of reproduction in whole or in part in any form.
ALADDIN is a trademark of Simon & Schuster, Inc., and related logo is
a registered trademark of Simon & Schuster, Inc.
For information about special discounts for bulk purchases, please contact
Simon & Schuster Special Sales at 1-866-506-1949 or business@simonandschuster.com.
The Simon & Schuster Speakers Bureau can bring authors to your live event. For more
information or to book an event, contact the Simon & Schuster Speakers Bureau
at 1-866-248-3049 or visit our website at www.simonspeakers.com.
Series design by Jeanine Henderson
Jacket design by Laura Lyn DiSiena
The text of this book was set in Adobe Caslon.
Manufactured in the United States of America 0116 FFG
10 9 8 7 6 5 4 3 2 1
Library of Congress Control Number 2015954051
ISBN 978-1-4814-2394-6 (hc)
ISBN 978-1-4814-2393-9 (pbk)
ISBN 978-1-4814-2395-3 (eBook)

For my nephew Jonah Ari May.

May your life be filled with love (and sparkles)!

Tons of love and glittery thanks to

Karen Nagel, Miriam Altshuler, Marianna Baer,

Eliot Schrefer, and Marie Rutkoski.

Contents

Wedding Bell Blues

one

Really Rosie

Aly Tanner was up to her elbows in suds. Her sister, Brooke, had tipped some extra soap into the pedicure basin, and now there were way more bubbles than usual covering Annie Wu's feet.

Brooke looked over from the pedicure she was giving to Annie's stepsister, Jayden Smith. "Oh no! I think I might have overdone it with the bubbles!" she said, laughing. "Sorry, Aly."

Aly smiled at her sister. A few too many bubbles never hurt anyone.

"Can you overdo it for me too?" Jayden asked. She was a first grader and visited the Sparkle Spa pretty often.

Aly pulled one of her hands out of the water and leaned over to add more soap to Jayden's basin. Soon Brooke had bubbles up to her elbows as well.

"Hey!" Brooke said as the lather kept growing.

Jayden started laughing. Annie, too.

"I know this might not be the best business plan," Brooke said to Aly, "because it'll mean we need to buy more soap solution. But if it makes our customers laugh, maybe we should *always* add extra bubbles."

Aly laughed at the idea of the Sparkle Spa covered in bubbles. "Let's see how much it would cost, Brookester," she said.

Aly and Brooke were the co–chief executive officers of the Sparkle Spa—they were in charge of the salon and everything that happened in it. That included bubble purchasing.

"Did you girls choose colors yet?" Charlotte asked Annie and Jayden.

Charlotte was a fifth grader, like Aly, and one of Aly's two best friends. She was also the chief operating officer of the Sparkle Spa and made sure the spa ran smoothly and was organized.

"I did," Annie and Jayden said at the same time, holding up their nail polish bottles. Annie's was a bright red called Really Rosie, and Jadyen's was a dark blue called Good Knight.

Charlotte looked at her clipboard and at the girls sitting in the jewelry-making area. "Hannah's missing," she said to Aly.

"I forgot to tell you," Aly answered. "Hannah had to cancel her appointment. Her phone was taken away in music class, and she needed to wait at school until one of her parents could come to get it back."

"Oh no," Sophie said. She was Brooke's best friend and the only other third grader who worked at the Sparkle Spa. She was a manicurist—a really good one—and was in the middle of a sparkly Lemon Aid manicure on a fourth grader named Eliza.

As Aly lifted Annie's feet out of the warm water, she looked around the Sparkle Spa and smiled. When she and Brooke had started the salon at the beginning of the school year, they had no idea how awesome it was going to be, with so many kids coming by to get their nails done, and then staying because it was fun to hang out.

Before Aly could open the Really Rosie polish, there was a knock against the door frame that led from True Colors, Aly and Brooke's mom's nail salon, into the Sparkle Spa in the back room.

"Hello?" a man's voice said.

Aly turned around quickly. Brooke turned too, and when she saw who it was, she jumped up. "Isaac!" she screeched, and ran over to him.

Isaac was a local photographer who'd taken pictures of Sparkle Spa events. He'd been visiting True Colors a lot recently because he was dating Joan, Aly and Brooke's favorite manicurist and their mom's best friend.

"Hi, Isaac," Aly said. "Does Mom need us?"

Isaac cleared his throat. "Actually," he said, "*I* need your help." Then he noticed the Sparkle Spa customers and employees. "Everyone's help, if you wouldn't mind."

Aly turned to Annie. "Could you hold on a sec?" she asked, walking over to Brooke and Isaac. Isaac rubbed his hand over the stubble on his chin, like he was nervous about something. "What's going on?" she asked.

Isaac kept rubbing his chin. "I need you to help me with a surprise," he said, "for Joan."

Brooke tugged on her braid. "I love surprises!" she said. "What do you want to do? Throw her a party? Get her a present? And how can we help? Do you need us to distract her? We can be very distracting. Sparkly, too." Brooke nodded at Sparkly, the girls' dog, who was sleeping in a corner of the salon. "Well, we might have to wake him up first."

Isaac spoke quietly. "I want to ask her to marry me."

Aly's mouth dropped open. Joan? Getting married? To Isaac?

"What?!" Brooke shrieked. "This is so exciting! I've never been to a wedding before!" Then she turned to Aly. "Did you hear? There's going to be a wedding! We're going to get to wear the most gorgeous dresses with high heels!"

Aly laughed. "I didn't hear Isaac say any of that. But he did say he needs our help."

"Right," Isaac said. "If it's okay with you, I'd like to propose to Joan in the Sparkle Spa. I have pictures I'd like you to hang up on ribbons. We can spread rose petals all over the floor. And when everything's ready, you can make up a reason for her to come back here and—"

"And you'll get down on one knee and tell her you'll love her forever and ever and give her a big, sparkly ring!" Brooke said.

By now, the rest of the girls in the Sparkle Spa were listening in on the conversation.

"Is that what's going to happen?" Jayden asked, splashing her feet in the bubbles.

Isaac cleared his throat. "Something like that," he said, gazing around the busy room. "I think I should have mentioned my plan sooner than today," he said to Aly and Brooke. "I didn't realize how many customers you'd have in here."

Aly turned to Brooke. Isaac was right. She really wanted to help him out and was excited he was going to ask Joan—their favorite Joan!—to marry him. But she and Brooke were busy running a business. Could they possibly postpone all of their appointments to make this happen?

Aly sent Brooke a Secret Sister Eye Message: *Can we do this?*

Brooke sent her one back: *How can we not?*

And Aly knew her sister was right. She just hoped their customers would understand.

two

As Red as It Gets

Aly gathered the Sparkle Spa customers around the pedicure chairs and explained what was going on, even though most of them had already overheard.

"So we're really sorry times a million, but we have to cancel the rest of today's appointments," Brooke announced.

"And we can reschedule you for Sunday or anytime next week," Aly finished. "Just talk to Charlotte."

Aly held her breath. She was worried that their

customers might be mad, and she hated when people were mad. Especially at her. She grew even more worried when nobody said anything at first. But then Annie spoke up. "Can we help?"

Aly tucked her hair behind her ear. "With what?" she asked.

"With the setup!" Annie said. "I've never been part of a marriage proposal before. It sounds like fun."

"Me too!" said Jayden. "I want to help."

"And me," said Eliza. "If you could use another person."

Soon everyone in the spa had volunteered to help. No one was angry about their appointments being canceled.

Aly ran over to Isaac, who had been waiting by the Sparkle Spa's polish wall. "Okay," she said. "We'll all help. Just tell us what you need."

Isaac pulled out a stack of photos from his camera

bag. There were pictures of him and Joan hiking, ski-
ing, walking through a museum, blowing out birth-
day candles. They were all black-and-white shots with
a single color added to each one, as if Isaac had painted
it on. In one Joan had really red lips. In another Isaac's
tie was neon blue.

"These are so cool," Brooke said.

Aly thought so too. She especially liked the photo
where Joan and Isaac were feeding ducks, and all of
the ducks were bright yellow.

But Isaac wasn't paying attention to what the girls
were saying. He was digging around in his camera
bag. When he brought his hand out this time, he was
holding a skein of ribbon and some clear tape.

"Okay," he said, "I was hoping you could cut the
ribbon and attach it to the pictures, then hang the ribbons all over the salon. I'm going to run out and pick
up the rose petals for the floor. Sound like a plan?"

"Aye, aye, Isaac," Brooke said, saluting him.

"No problem at all," Aly said, glad so many friends were helping them. This seemed like a pretty big project, actually. Isaac really should have asked them sooner. Aly could have at least precut the ribbon!

While Isaac was gone, the girls cut, taped, and hung fifty-five pictures. Lily, Aly's other best friend and the salon's chief financial officer, had counted each one and made sure they were placed perfectly around the room.

Charlotte was admiring a shot of Joan and Isaac standing on a mountaintop, a bright green backpack on Joan's back. "This is so romantic," she said with a sigh.

Aly agreed.

Isaac burst through the salon's back door, holding

up bags of rose petals. "I've got them, girls." He stopped in his tracks. "Wow," he said. "This looks even better than I'd imagined it would. Joan's going to flip!"

He handed the petals to Aly, Sophie, and Brooke, and the three of them carefully spread handfuls on the floor. When they were finished, the girls couldn't believe how magical the back room looked. Even Sparkly barked his approval.

"Okay," Charlotte said, "I think our work here is done. Everyone except Aly and Brooke should probably leave. But make sure to come back for your new appointments."

"Again, we're sorry again for canceling," Aly added.

"No problem at all," Annie said. "This was so much cooler than having my toes polished."

"Are you ready?" Brooke asked Isaac when

everyone was gone. "Because I don't think I can wait a minute more."

Aly felt the same way. She had never seen anyone proposed to in real life, only on TV.

Once again, Isaac rubbed his chin. "I'm as ready as I'll ever be. Let's do this!" he said. "Can one of you ask Joan to come back here?"

"I'll do it!" both girls said at once.

"We'll both go," Aly said. She was trying not to feel nervous, but so much excitement bubbled up inside her.

The sisters walked into True Colors, not paying any attention to the customers or even to their mom, who was at manicure station number one, giving Mrs. Franklin a French manicure.

"Joanie!" Brooke said, running over to Joan's regular station, number seven. "We need you in the Sparkle Spa."

Joan looked up from Mrs. Howard's As Red as It Gets manicure. "Is everything okay?" she asked.

Aly nodded. She felt like she needed to come up with an excuse so Joan wouldn't get alarmed. "We just . . . we just . . ."

"We made a really cool design on the nail polish wall that we want to show you," Brooke said.

"When you're done with Mrs. Howard," Aly added.

Joan smiled. "Well then, you're in luck," she said, "because all I have to do is three more fingers of top coat and Mrs. Howard will be ready to dry."

Aly watched Brooke tug her braid; it made her wish she had one to tug. She couldn't wait to see Joan's reaction.

A minute or so later—which seemed like forever—Joan got up and walked with the girls to the Sparkle Spa. When they got to the door, Aly said, "Joan, why don't you go in first, so you can see the, um, pattern we made right away."

Joan gave Aly a funny look, but she walked ahead anyway. Then she gasped. "Isaac," she said. "What's . . . what's going on?"

Aly and Brooke watched as Isaac got down on one knee, opened a ring box, and asked Joan to marry him.

At first Joan didn't say anything. Aly held her breath. Brooke tugged on her braid.

And then Joan answered. "Yes! Yes! Yes!"

Isaac stood up, and they kissed, just like they were on TV.

Aly started clapping, and Brooke started cheering. Before they knew it, everyone else in True Colors had joined them.

Aly turned around, surprised to see Mom standing behind her, eyes dripping quiet tears. "Isn't this beautiful?" she asked Aly.

"Do you think we're going to get to be flower girls?" Brooke whispered to Mom. "And do you think Sparkly's going to get to be a flower dog? He'd look great in a dog tutu."

Mom shrugged her shoulders and smiled mysteriously. "I think you'll find out soon enough."

"I hope both things come true!" Brooke said.

Aly wasn't so sure. She'd never heard of anyone having a flower dog before. And as a fifth grader, she thought she might be a little too old to be a flower girl.

three

Peaches and Dreams

The night after she became engaged, Joan called the Tanner house. Brooke picked up the phone and started right in asking Joan what she thought about dogs wearing tutus: Were they cute? Was pink the best dog tutu color? But instead of answering like she usually would, Joan asked if she could talk to Mom. She promised Brooke that they could have a very long conversation about dog tutus in the salon later that week.

"Sure thing," Brooke said, putting Joan on speaker.

"The dog tutus can wait. I'll go get Mom." Then she yelled, *"Mooooooom! Phooooone! It's Joooooooan!"*

"That doesn't sound quite like getting her to me," Joan said with a laugh on the other end.

"Close enough," Brooke told her.

Mom didn't pick up, so Aly went to find her. She walked upstairs and poked her head into her parents' bedroom. Mom was there, talking on her cell phone.

"Hey," Aly whispered. "Joan's on the phone."

"Tell her I'll call her back, sweetie," Mom said. "I'm on with Dad."

Aly nodded. Dad traveled a lot for work and usually came home on Friday nights. But he was on an especially long trip this time and wouldn't be making it home for the weekend. She wanted to say hi to him, but it seemed like Mom had some more important things to talk about, so Aly quietly left the room.

✳ ✳ ✳ ✳ ✳

The girls went to bed that night thinking about Joan and her wedding.

"Do you think there's anyone else she could possibly ask to be her flower girls?" Brooke said from her side of the room.

Aly rolled over to face her sister. "I don't know. Maybe she isn't planning on having flower girls. Or maybe Isaac has people to ask."

Brooke gasped. "Isaac's people! I hadn't thought of that."

"But Joan loves us," Aly added. "So she'll probably pick us."

"Probably," Brooke repeated.

Aly still wasn't sure how she felt about being a flower girl. All the flower girls she'd seen were three or five or maybe seven years old. She was ten and Brooke was eight. Was there an age limit?

* * * * *

The next morning Mom woke the girls up earlier than usual. "Rise and shine!" she said. "I spoke to Joan last night after you two fell asleep. She asked me to bring you to the bridal shop today."

Aly stretched and rubbed the sleep out of her eyes.

"Does Joan want us to come because we're going to be flower girls?" Brooke asked.

Mom just smiled. "She asked me to be her matron of honor, but she didn't mention anything about you two. She also asked me to figure out a way to donate the extra food from her wedding to a charity in town. I'm going to have to do some research on that today. Maybe you girls can help."

"We're going to be flower girls, and Sparkly's going to be the flower dog—I just know it, " Brooke said, getting out of bed and sliding on her glasses.

"Of course we can help," Aly told her mom. But

she wasn't really thinking about the food donation. She was thinking that ten years old was practically eleven, which was really close to being a teenager. And teenagers were never flower girls.

"Maybe Joan wants us to help her choose her dress," Aly offered. "Or choose the color for her bridesmaids. We're very good color pickers."

Brooke nodded. "That's true, we are. But we could do those things *and* be her flower girls."

Brooke had a point. Then again, Brooke *always* had a point.

When they entered the Something New bridal shop, Aly couldn't believe her eyes. One side of the shop was filled with hundreds of dresses in hundreds of different colors—more colors than all of the nail polishes in the whole Sparkle Spa—and the other side was lined with the whitest, poofiest dresses she had ever seen.

"Hi, girls," Joan greeted them. They both gave her a hug. "My appointment is in this room to the right."

Brooke and Aly followed Joan, and for the second time in two minutes, Aly couldn't believe her eyes. There, sitting on a couch, surrounded by dresses and books filled with fabric samples, were Suzy Davis and her younger sister, Heather, who was sitting on Isaac's lap.

"*Suzy?*" Aly said.

Suzy looked up from a bridal magazine. "Hi," she said.

"Did you know I was going to be here?" Aly asked.

Suzy shrugged. "I guessed it. I knew Uncle Isaac was dating your mom's best friend."

Aly couldn't believe her ears. "Why didn't you say anything?" she said. Then she turned to Joan and her mom. "Why didn't anyone say anything?"

Suzy and Aly were on speaking terms now, but

that hadn't always been the case. Suzy had been mean to Aly for years and had almost destroyed the Sparkle Spa a couple months ago. After the school carnival last month, the girls decided they didn't hate each other anymore, but still. It wasn't like they hung out all the time. Or ever, really.

"I didn't meet Isaac's brother and his family until last week," Joan said.

"And I didn't make the connection until I spoke to Joan last night," Mom said.

Mom had not been a big fan of Suzy Davis either, but the carnival had changed her mind a little.

There was a lull in the conversation. Brooke looked at Aly and sent her a Secret Sister Eye Message: *Can you believe this?*

Aly sent her one back: *Something bad is going to happen. I can feel it.*

Heather moved off of Isaac's lap. Standing up,

he said, "How about all of you girls gather together over here. Joan and I have something important to ask you."

Aly felt Brooke grab her hand. They walked over and sat on the couch between Heather and Suzy.

Suzy immediately slid closer to Aly, even though there was plenty of room on her side. Aly sighed.

"So," Joan said, "we know this is a little out of the ordinary, but we'd love to have all four of you as our flower girls."

Brooke and Heather squealed.

Joan continued. "We haven't picked the color yet, but I just fell in love with this flower girl dress. We'll order it in each of your sizes in whatever color we choose."

She lifted up a dress the color of Peaches and Dreams nail polish that had poofy sleeves with ruffles and a huge bow at the waist. Aly thought it was pretty, but she also thought it looked like a little-girl dress. She was not thrilled at the idea of wearing it, but she loved Joan, so . . .

"We're too old," Suzy said, breaking into Aly's thoughts. "Aly and me, we're too old to be flower girls. And that's a baby dress, no offense. We're both almost eleven, which is too old to wear a baby dress. Right, Aly?" Suzy crossed her arms and looked at Aly.

"Well . . . ," Aly began. Suzy wasn't wrong, but Aly didn't want to hurt Joan's feelings.

"See?" Suzy said. "Aly agrees. And since we're so good at making people beautiful, we're going to have a different job at the wedding. We're going to be Brooke and Heather's stylists. We'll do their nails and their makeup and their hair. That's a more grown-up job."

Brooke looked at Aly.

Joan looked at Aly.

Mom looked at Joan.

Joan looked at Isaac.

Isaac looked at Suzy.

"If that's what you want, that's fine with me," he said.

Suzy smiled and said, "Thanks, Uncle Isaac."

"Are you sure that's what *you* want?" Mom asked Aly.

Aly froze. She didn't know how to answer, so many thoughts were going through her mind:

1. Suzy was right—the dress was for little kids.
2. A stylist did sound like a more fun, grown-up job.
3. Aly had felt all along that she was too old to be a flower girl.

4. But a flower girl was a real part of the wedding.

5. A stylist was not. A stylist didn't get to walk down the aisle and wear the wedding colors.

6. But that might be better than wearing a baby dress down the aisle for everyone at the wedding to see.

"I—I—I'm . . . ," Aly stammered.

"She's sure," Suzy said. "We're *not* babies."

"Neither are we," Brooke snapped. "The dress is beautiful."

Aly nodded her head weakly. "Being a stylist will be fun," she said.

Joan looked at Aly again. "Okay," she said, "I'm sure it will."

"So," Brooke said, "is there any chance Sparkly can be the flower dog?"

The grown-ups laughed, and Aly felt relieved that there was a new topic of conversation. But she also felt worried that she might have just made a big mistake she wouldn't be able to fix.

four
Midnight Blues

That night, after Aly and Brooke had helped Mom make phone calls to local charities in the afternoon, hoping to find one that could make good use of the food that would be left over from the wedding (they did—it was called Rock & Wrap It Up), Aly sat on Brooke's bed, braiding her sister's hair. Her own hair was a little too short for braiding.

"Is this the kind of hairstyle you're going to give me for Joan's wedding?" Brooke asked. The braid crossed her head, starting at her left temple and ending just over her right shoulder.

"I don't think so," Aly answered. "This isn't fancy enough. Maybe we should look at some flower girl hairdos in magazines or online."

Aly wrapped an elastic the color of Midnight Blues polish around the bottom of the braid. "Let's check Mom's computer," Brooke said.

The girls went into the home office. Aly wiggled the mouse to wake up the computer, then did a search for "flower girl hair images."

Hundreds of pictures came up. Aly and Brooke scanned them all.

"*Oooh!*" Brooke cooed. "Look at *that* one!"

A lot of the styles were just half-up hairdos with curls, but the one Brooke was pointing to looked really complicated: A big bun sat on top, with two braids coming in from the sides and curls falling down the back. Around the bun was a crown of flowers.

"I like it, Brookester," Aly said. "We'll have to ask Joan about the flower crown, but I think I can figure out how to do the rest of it."

"That's awesome," Brooke said. "I'm going to look like a flower princess."

"You totally are," Aly agreed.

Brooke was quiet for a moment before she asked, "Are you sure you don't want to be a flower girl? Because I'd rather be a flower girl with you than with Heather Davis. You're my sister, and she's just a first grader. You and I do things better when we're a team."

Aly hugged her sister. If she had spoken right then, Brooke might have heard the tears in her voice. Sometimes the weirdest things made Aly feel like she was going to cry.

"I like being a team with you too," she said, "and

if Suzy weren't involved, I probably would be a flower girl. But you know what's most annoying about Suzy Davis? Even when she's mean about things, she's right a lot of the time. Look at all the girls in these photos." Aly pointed to the screen. "The oldest one looks nine. Almost eleven really does feel too old to be a flower girl."

Brooke pushed her glasses up on her nose and sighed. "I just wish that you were going to be in the wedding with me and that we could walk down the aisle together wearing fancy dresses."

Aly wished that too. "I'm sure I'll wear a fancy dress," she said. "I'm still coming to the wedding, and even regular guests need nice clothes for weddings. I just won't get to walk down the aisle. But Dad won't either, so I guess I'll sit with him."

"But don't you *want* to walk down the aisle?" Brooke asked.

"I kind of do."

Aly must've looked sad, because Brooke started stroking her hair. "Don't worry, Al," she said. "I'll tell you what it's like. And this way, you'll get to make me look extra beautiful for the wedding. That'll be a lot of fun, right?"

"Right," Aly said, grinning. "Okay, let's head back to our room to see if I can get your hair to look like that."

But as she unbraided and rebraided Brooke's hair, all Aly could think about was watching her sister from the wedding sidelines.

five

Green Tease

On Sunday, Aly was pretty quiet at the Sparkle Spa. Joan didn't seem her usual self either.

"Don't you think Joanie should be happier, since she's getting married?" Brooke asked Aly. She was giving Daisy Quinn, a sixth grader, a polka-dot manicure. "If I were planning a wedding with someone as nice as Isaac, I'd be the happiest person on the whole planet."

Aly just shrugged. She was giving Daisy's younger sister Violet a stars-and-stripes manicure. She was finding it hard to concentrate on the stripes, worrying that Joan was sad because Aly wasn't going to be one of her flower girls.

"Maybe the person doesn't really want to get married," Daisy offered.

Aly shook her head. "I don't think that's it," she said. But as she painted stripes on Violet's pinkies, she had to wonder.

After the girls finished their appointments for the day, they cleaned up, which included wiping up a giant spill of the new color Green Tease. One of their customers, Uma Prasad, had accidentally knocked over the bottle with her elbow. Nobody had realized until it was too late.

Aly was on her knees, using nail polish remover on the linoleum floor, when Mom and Joan walked in. "Aly," she said, "do you remember what Rock & Wrap

It Up told us about the donations? I left the paper with all the information at home."

Aly's list was at home too, but she closed her eyes and tried to recall what was on it. They'd put the phone on speaker when they'd called the various charities, and Aly had taken notes—mostly because having lists helped her make decisions, and she wanted to help Mom make the right one about Joan's wedding. Aly could picture what she'd written in purple glitter pen on a mint-green piece of paper:

Rock & Wrap It Up Donation
Information
- Food that has been on anyone's plate cannot be donated.
- All hot food has to stay at a safe temperature between the time of the wedding and pickup time.

- Same with cold food.
- Everything has to be wrapped up in advance by people who know about food safety.
- The donation truck will arrive fifteen minutes after the reception ends.

"Thanks, sweetie," her mom said after Aly recited each item. "I knew it was good to have you two on the phone with me."

"Thanks, kiddo," Joan said. "You girls gave me the idea for this donation because of your policy at the Sparkle Spa. There is always so much extra food at a wedding, and I hated the idea of throwing it out."

"You're doing it because of us?" Brooke asked. She had flopped on the pillows in the waiting area.

"Well, I thought if you girls could donate all of

your profits to charity, the least I could do was donate my extra wedding food."

"Maybe the next time our strawberry donation jar is full," Aly said, thinking out loud, "we could donate the money to Rock & Wrap It Up. What do you think, Brookester?"

"I like it," Brooke said.

Joan walked over and put her arm around Aly's shoulders. "You're a good kid, Aly," she said. "I hope you don't let Isaac's niece push you around."

Aly leaned into Joan. Had she been letting Suzy Davis push her around? That was a definite possibility.

The next day at school Aly was sitting at her usual lunch table, Charlotte next to her and Lily across from them. Just as she bit into a Granny Smith apple, Suzy came by.

"I have so many ideas about Heather and Brooke's makeup and nails," she said to Aly. "I know the Sparkle Spa's not open today, so I was thinking we should get together to talk about it. You can come to my house after school."

"Even when the Sparkle Spa's not open," Aly replied, "I usually stop by to help out at True Colors. My mom's expecting me."

Suzy rolled her eyes. "So call her and tell her you can't. Don't you think Joan and Uncle Isaac's wedding is a little more important that reorganizing a dumb polish wall?"

Aly sighed. "Okay," she said. "I'll call her." But as she said those words, Aly wondered if this is what Joan meant about letting Suzy Davis push her around.

"Good," Suzy said. "Meet me in front of the school after the last bell. My babysitter will be there in a red car."

"Red car," Aly repeated. "Got it." She'd have to find Brooke and make sure she had someone else to walk with her to True Colors. Or maybe Suzy's babysitter could give her a ride. Either way, Brooke wasn't allowed to walk to the salon from school alone, so Aly had to figure out a backup plan. Suzy Davis was complicating everything!

Once Suzy walked away, Charlotte asked, "What was that about?"

"I think it's about me messing up. Big-time," Aly said. "Joan asked me and Brooke and Suzy and Heather to be flower girls, and then Suzy said the two of us were too old. I agreed."

"I know," Lily said. "You told us about it yesterday."

"Right," Charlotte said, "and you *are* too old. I was a flower girl when I was four. Suzy may be mean, but she's not dumb. And you said the dress was way too young."

"Well, Suzy also decided that she and I would be Brooke and Heather's stylists for the wedding. I didn't get a chance to tell you that yesterday."

"That sounds like fun!" Charlotte said.

Aly took a sip of juice. "It does," she said. "But . . . but . . . I really wish I were in the wedding instead. Even if it means being the oldest flower girl ever."

"Maybe you could come up with something else to do," Lily suggested. "Think of all the jobs there are at the Sparkle Spa—there must be even more for a wedding."

"Like what?" Aly asked. She pulled a pen out of her pocket and spread her napkin out on the table, ready to make one of her lists.

"Well, there's the bride," Lily said, "and the groom."

Charlotte broke off a piece of her vanilla cookie with M&M's on top. "Aly can't be the bride or groom, Lily."

"I know, I know," Lily said. "I was just getting warmed up. Um, how about ring bearer?"

"That's for little kids too," Aly said.

"And usually boys," Charlotte added through a mouthful of cookie. "Caleb was the ring bearer when I was the flower girl at our aunt's wedding."

"Bridesmaid?" Lily said.

"For grown-ups," Charlotte responded.

"Groomsman?" Lily said.

"Also grown-ups," Aly told her.

"Were there any other jobs at your aunt's wedding?" Lily asked Charlotte.

Charlotte took another bite. "My older cousin Stacey gave out programs. Maybe you could do that, Aly."

Aly was intrigued. "Did she get to walk down the aisle?"

Charlotte shook her head.

"Then I don't want that one either."

All three friends stared at one another. Then Lily finally said, "Maybe you should just talk to Joan again about being a flower girl."

"I don't think that's an option anymore," Aly muttered. "I think I'm going to have to be a stylist and that's that."

The girls finished eating and started walking back to class. Charlotte put her arm around Aly's shoulders. "Well, at least you'll get a nice dress. Maybe Lily and I can go shopping with you."

For the first time that day, Aly smiled. That *would* be fun. And the wedding was about Joan and Isaac, after all. She had to start focusing on them—she'd try, anyway.

Six
Yellow, Sunshine!

From the start, the afternoon didn't go smoothly.

Brooke wanted to come to Suzy's house too, so she could offer her own ideas about her flower girl look.

Aly shrugged in response. "Fine with me. You're the one we're styling."

But then Suzy said no. "Your sister is *not* the stylist. *We* are the stylists."

Aly thought once more about what Joan had said. She put her hands on her hips and spoke firmly.

"She's my sister, and if she wants to come, she gets to come. Besides, she always has good ideas. We make a good team."

"But it's *my* house," Suzy said, her own hands on her hips. "And you and I are the team here."

Brooke narrowed her eyes and watched the exchange, moving her head from Aly to Suzy and back.

"We should actually meet in the Sparkle Spa," Aly said. "That's where the nail polish is."

"The meeting's at *my* house," Suzy insisted. "That was the plan. I have makeup and hair accessories there. Plus, you know how I feel about the Sparkle Spa. Small and smelly."

Brooke took a big step to stand right in front of Suzy. "For the very last time," she said, "the Sparkle Spa *does not smell*! And if you're going to insult our salon, I don't want you to style me."

Suzy huffed. "It's my *job*," she argued.

Aly tucked her hair behind her ear. It fell back into her eye as she quietly told Suzy, "You know, you're the one who gave us that job. And it's not even a real wedding job. But if we're going to take it seriously, then we should probably test makeup colors and hairdos on Brooke and Heather."

Suzy played with the straps on her backpack. "Fine," she answered. "I guess you can come to my house, Brooke. And we can all talk about how a flower girl should look."

At that, the girls got into Suzy's babysitter's car. They stopped off at the Sparkle Spa so Aly could tell her mother about the change in plans and make arrangements to have Mom pick the girls up on her way home.

At Suzy's house things went from bad to worse. Suzy's babysitter gave the girls granola bars, and Brooke didn't like them because they had pistachios inside. Then the sitter gave them milk with ice cubes, and Aly thought that was too weird to drink. After that the girls went to Suzy's room to start making plans.

Suzy sat down on her bed, which was big and ruffle-y and had a lace canopy the color of Yellow, Sunshine! nail polish. Heather plopped into a watermelon-colored beanbag chair. Aly and Brooke took a seat on the thick rug with a yellow and pink zigzag pattern, the softest rug Aly had ever touched.

"Aly and I already picked how I want to wear my hair," Brooke said, leaning against Suzy's bookshelf. "Want to show them, Aly?"

Aly started loosely braiding and twisting Brooke's hair, holding it in place to show the girls how it would look.

Suzy scrunched her nose. "I don't know if I like it," she said. "It's very . . . up. Besides, you shouldn't have picked anything without me. I should have had a say."

Aly wasn't sure what the problem was with "up." In the pictures online, lots of flower girls wore their hair up. But she did see Suzy's other point. "We weren't planning on choosing a style without you . . . it just happened when we were looking online."

Then Heather, who had been sitting quietly, playing with the seams of the beanbag chair, piped up. "I want to wear my hair loose for Uncle Isaac's wedding. With a headband. Headbands are my favorite."

Now it was Brooke's turn to scrunch her nose. "Headbands are hard for me because of my glasses," she said. "See?" She turned to show Heather how the earpieces of her glasses tucked right behind her ears. "That's where a headband would go too. So the backs of my ears get sore when I try to wear one for long."

Aly tried to think of a compromise. "How about if

we make a braid that *looks* like a headband, and then the hair hangs loose in the back?"

Suzy crossed her arms. "The whole point of a headband is that it's sparkly and pretty on top of your head. A braid isn't sparkly or pretty."

"We can weave beads or ribbons into the braid?" Aly suggested.

Brooke was glaring at Aly, trying to send her a Secret Sister Eye Message, but Aly was looking at Suzy instead. Finally, Brooke blurted out, "But I want my hair up!"

Now Heather glared at Brooke. "And I want my hair down."

"*You* don't get to choose," Suzy said to her sister— and to Brooke, too. "Aly and I choose because we're the stylists."

Aly didn't like where this was going. She was pretty sure that part of being a stylist was making your clients happy with how they looked.

"You know," Aly began, "maybe Brooke and Heather can each have their own hairdo. They don't necessarily have to match."

Brooke's eyes lit up. "It's true!" she said. "We're just flower girls together. Not identical twins. Heather doesn't wear glasses, so we wouldn't look exactly the same anyway."

"Right, you won't look exactly the same, so you don't have to have the exact same hairstyle," Aly continued. "Wearing the same dress will be enough."

"I want to wear my gold sandals from the gala," Brooke told Aly. "Mom said I could, no matter what my dress looked like."

"And I have sparkly sandals that I wore when I was Cinderella for a fancy Halloween party," Heather said. "Remember, Suzy? I want to wear those."

Suzy was sitting on her bed quietly. Aly thought that could only mean trouble.

Brooke stood up. "Okay. No matching hair. No matching shoes. Time to talk about makeup."

Aly loved how her sister could go from upset to excited in seconds.

She stood up now too. "I think Brooke's right. Let's look at makeup. That's your specialty, right, Suzy? If we're done with hair, you can show us your ideas."

Suzy didn't say anything for a second. Then she slid off her bed and started walking across her room. "Yep, we're done with hair. So let's move this along."

For special occasions Suzy ran a business she had named Suzy's Spectacular Makeup. Even though Aly and Brooke weren't fans of the idea at first, they ended up liking it a lot. Suzy had even worked with them at the school carnival to make the Sparkle Spa booth extra successful.

"Would you like to see my special makeup case?" Suzy asked, walking over to a vanity in the corner of her bedroom. "You can't touch it, though."

She held up her beautiful makeup case decorated with glittery stickers. *Suzy* was written in script with shimmering Go for the Gold nail polish.

As she slowly opened the case, the girls could see all kinds of sparkly products inside: glittery eye shadow in silver and gold, fairy dust powder for cheeks, lip gloss in six different colors.

"Let's get to testing," she said. "But I'm the only one who gets to use the makeup."

Aly rolled her eyes, but agreed. Heather went first.

Suzy must have practiced on her sister before, because Heather didn't blink an eye when Suzy brushed silver eye shadow on her lids and applied hot-pink shimmer gloss to her lips.

When it was Brooke's turn, she was much more squirmy and ticklish.

"Stop moving around so much," Suzy ordered, "or I'll poke you in the eye."

Suzy chose gold eye shadow and a light pink gloss for Brooke—quite different from Heather's look.

In the end, everyone agreed that *not* matching was a better plan.

Heather and Brooke couldn't stop looking at themselves in the vanity mirror.

"We look gorgeous, don't we?" Heather squealed.

Aly had to agree—Suzy had done a good job. "What about their nails?" she asked now.

Brooke replied, "It's better to choose polishes at the Sparkle Spa."

"And not until after we know exactly what color the dresses are," Suzy said.

"When are we finding that out?" Aly asked. "Has Isaac told you yet?"

"Saturday," Heather said as the girls started walking downstairs. "We're all supposed to go back to the dress store on Saturday to see if our dresses fit. That's when we'll get to see the surprise color."

That gave Aly an idea. "How about if I bring a case of nail polishes to the bridal store? We can pick out a color right there."

"Great idea," Heather said.

"Yes," Suzy added. By this time, they were near the front door. "That's actually a good one."

Wow, Aly thought. *Almost a compliment from Suzy!* "Okay then," she said. "It's a plan."

Waiting outside for their mom to come, Aly breathed a sigh of relief. Thankfully, the afternoon had ended up much better than it had started.

Aly had been so pleased with how Brooke and

Heather looked, she'd forgotten for a moment that *she* wasn't going to be wearing makeup and walking down the aisle.

But now . . . now she was more determined than ever to figure out a way to make that happen. Just not in a frilly, poofy dress.

seven

Pretty in Pink

On Saturday morning the Tanner women headed back to Something New. They left the house as quietly as they could so they wouldn't wake Dad—he had come home late Friday night and had told Mom that he was looking forward to sleeping in today and seeing the girls after their dress shopping.

As the Tanner women walked to the car, Mom filled them in on where things stood: Yes, the flower girl dresses had come in, and Brooke and Heather would be able to try them on today to make sure they fit. If they didn't fit, the bridal shop could make alterations. Mom's matron of honor dress had come in too. Joan had picked the colors last weekend, but since she wanted to surprise everyone, she'd kept them a secret.

Aly's rolling suitcase was filled with every single nail polish color the Sparkle Spa had in stock. She'd be prepared no matter what colors Joan had chosen!

"I can't wait, I can't wait, I can't wait!" Brooke chanted as they loaded the suitcase into the car. "Mom, did Joan really not tell you the color of my dress? Not even a hint?"

"Not even a hint," Mom said, laughing. This conversation had been going on for days, and Mom's answer was always the same. Aly figured either she *really* didn't know or she was a fantastic pretender.

Walking into the bridal shop was just as magical as it had been the first time they'd been there. It even smelled liked a wedding.

Ralph from Rock & Wrap It Up was there talking to Joan. "Thanks, Joan," he was saying. "That sounds like a plan."

Brooke flew across the room to Joan. "*What* are the colors? *Where* are the dresses?"

Joan dropped a kiss on the top of Brooke's head. "I need one more minute with Ralph, sweetie, and then I'll show you."

Brooke tugged on her braid and stayed right next to Joan while she finished talking to Ralph. Aly, on the other hand, parked her suitcase of polish next to a See Coral–colored chair and wandered around the store looking at all the beautiful dresses. Some were extra special with beads woven into the fabric and flowers embroidered on the skirt. Aly sighed and wished she could wear one of them.

When Aly had asked Mom last week if she could get a new dress for Joan's wedding, Mom had said no. She could wear the dress she wore for the

Businesswomen Unite gala. It was a beautiful dress and Aly loved it, but it wasn't quite as nice as these. Aly was certain that if she were walking down the aisle, she'd get a new dress.

Aly was carefully touching the See You Jader-colored beads on one of the dresses when a door next to her opened. Aly turned to see Joelle Hoffman walking out of a dressing room in a purple one-shouldered dress.

"Joelle!" Aly said. "What are you doing here?"

Joelle was one of the Auden Angels—the girls' soccer team at Aly's school—meaning she was one of the first Sparkle Spa customers. In fact, the Sparkle Spa had started because of the captain of the Angels, Jenica Posner. After Aly had given Jenica a rainbow sparkle pedicure, she'd played so well during her next soccer game that the whole team wanted the exact same pedicure. Now the Angels were some of the Sparkle Spa's most loyal customers.

"My stepsister's getting married," Joelle said. "And I'm a junior bridesmaid."

A *junior* bridesmaid—Aly had never head of that before. "What's a junior bridesmaid?"

"It's like a regular bridesmaid at a wedding," Joelle said, "but it's for someone who's not a grown-up. I'm wearing the same color as the adult bridesmaids, but a different dress. Theirs have no straps and mine has one. See?" Joelle turned so Aly could get a close-up view of the one shoulder strap. "Isn't it a cool dress?"

It *was.* There were two layers—the bottom was a shiny purple, and the top was a see-through purple. There was a beaded belt around the waist and beads dotting the back of the skirt.

A junior bridesmaid, Aly repeated to herself. Did Joan know what that was and would she possibly let Aly be one?

"My stepsister Carina chose it," Joelle went on.

"She picked out three options for me, and then I got to choose the dress I liked best."

"It looks fantastic," Aly told her. "Just the color of Give Me a Grape." Purple happened to be Aly's favorite color, along with green.

"Thanks," Joelle said. "Maybe I could get my fingers and toes done at the Sparkle Spa before the wedding."

"Of course," Aly said. "Just let me know when, and we'll make an appointment."

A tall girl with a purple streak in her hair came over to Joelle. "Let me see, Jo," she said.

Joelle spun around. "This is my friend Aly," she said. "Aly, this is Carina."

"Congratulations on your wedding," Aly said. "I like your hair."

"Thanks, Aly," Carina said. Then she turned to Joelle. "The dress looks perfect."

"I think so too," Aly said. "Hey, can I ask you a question?"

Joelle nodded.

"Are you walking down the aisle at Carina's wedding?"

"She sure is!" Carina answered. "And she'll even carry a bouquet of flowers."

"A purple bouquet," Joelle added.

"That sounds awesome," Aly said. One day she might like a purple-themed wedding of her own.

All this talk about Carina's wedding was nice, but Aly saw Ralph leave the store. She needed to get back to Joan, so Aly said good-bye to Joelle and hurried across the shop. "Joan, have you ever heard of . . . ," she started to say just as Isaac walked over with Suzy and Heather.

"Oh, there you are," Suzy said. "I was about to go looking for you. I thought maybe you got stuck under one of those poofy skirts or something. Ha!"

Aly smiled. "Not stuck," she said.

"Okay," Joan said, looking at everyone. "Now that you're all here, are you ready to find out the colors you'll be wearing?"

"I am!" Brooke squealed, bouncing on her toes.

"My flower girls," Joan said, "will be wearing pink with a turquoise sash."

"Pink!" Brooke said. "I was wishing for pink!"

"Me too!" cheered Heather.

"What shade of pink?" Aly asked.

Joan thought for a moment. "Like Pretty in Pink polish."

Brooke and Heather both clapped.

"And my bridesmaids—including my matron of honor—will be wearing turquoise."

Aly looked at her mom. Her mom was smiling.

"I knew you'd like that, Karen," Joan said.

At that moment one of the Something New saleswomen brought over the dresses.

"Joanie Baloney, these are the most scrumptious dresses ever. Aren't they, Heather?" Brooke said.

"I can't wait to try mine on," Heather exclaimed, grinning.

Aly was happy Brooke and Heather liked their dresses, even though they still looked too babyish to her. But Mom's turquoise dress was magnificent, with beads and flowers and a train trailing down the back of the gown. That decided it.

Even if it meant making Joan a little bit mad, Aly just had to have a beautiful turquoise dress like Mom's and walk down the aisle at Joan and Isaac's wedding. Aly swallowed hard. Was she really brave enough to ask?

eight

Turquoise Delight

Aly knew if she waited one more second, all her courage would disappear. She closed her eyes and blurted, "Joan, I really, *really* want to be a part of your wedding and walk down the aisle and wear a new dress. I just learned there's a job called 'junior bridesmaid.' May I please be one? I'm sorry if it causes trouble . . . but . . . but I just really want to be one. For you."

Suzy looked from Aly to Joan. Her eyes opened wide. "Me too!" she said. "If Aly gets to be one, I want to be one too."

Joan took a while to respond. Aly's stomach felt squishy and nervous.

"I don't know," Joan finally answered. "There aren't any junior groomsmen, so the numbers would be off. We're trying to keep things even on both sides. That's why I asked you two to be flower girls."

Aly looked down at the floor, trying not to cry. She thought she'd come up with the perfect plan. "It was just an idea," she squeaked out.

"Wait!" Suzy said. "I have another idea." She smiled at her uncle. "What if I'm a groomsgirl?"

"A groomsgirl?" he repeated, pulling his baseball cap off to scratch his head.

"What would that mean?" Joan asked.

Suzy cleared her throat. "Well, I'd wear the same exact dress as Aly, but I'd wear it in black so that I'd match all the groomsmen in their tuxedos! Then she and I could walk down the aisle together. Aly could stand with the bridesmaids, and I'd stand with the groomsmen. And then it would be balanced."

Isaac turned to Joan. "She did take care of the numbers issue," he said.

"Please?" Suzy said.

"Please?" Aly echoed.

Joan closed her eyes and took a deep breath.

Oh no, Aly worried. *Now I've ruined Joan's most special day ever. I've made her feel terrible.*

At last Joan opened her eyes. "Okay," she said. "You can be a junior bridesmaid and a groomsgirl."

Aly and Suzy looked at each other and smiled.

"Yes!" Suzy yelped.

Aly hugged Joan tightly. "Thank you so much," she whispered. "I really wanted to be in your wedding. I didn't really want to be a stylist."

"I know," Joan whispered back. Then she beckoned Suzy over. "You know, girls," she said, "Isaac and I were a little bit hurt when we invited you to be in our wedding and you said no."

Aly stared at her shoes again. She traced the path her sneaker laces made as they snaked in and out of the holes. "I'm sorry," she said.

Suzy didn't say anything.

"Suzy," Aly whispered.

"Fine," Suzy said. "I'm sorry too. It's just that we were too old—"

Aly cut her off. "She's sorry, Joan. We're both very sorry we made you and Isaac feel bad."

"Thank you," Joan said. "It takes someone very grown up and responsible to apologize."

Aly could hear Suzy huff next to her.

"So how about we find you two some beautiful grown-up dresses to wear?" Joan continued.

Aly wiped away the tears that were still lingering on her eyelashes. "Sounds good to me."

✳   ✳   ✳   ✳   ✳

Six dresses later, Aly was wearing a dress the color of Turquoise Delight—the exact shade as her mother's. The dress had a scooped neck and straps that criss-crossed in the back. A sash of turquoise flowers trailed down the back of the dress to the floor.

"What do you think?" Aly asked Suzy.

"Hmm," Suzy said. "I was hoping for a little bit of sparkle."

So far, the other five dresses had been rejected because:

1. Suzy didn't like dresses with short sleeves.
2. Aly didn't like dresses with long sleeves.
3. Mom didn't think the girls were old enough to go strapless.

4. Joan didn't want the girls in dresses made of shiny fabric.

5. Both Suzy and Aly refused to wear dresses with bows.

But Mom, Joan, and Aly all liked this dress. And Suzy seemed to like it too, except for the lack of sparkles.

"What if we do sparkly nails?" Aly offered. "With sparkly makeup. And maybe we could even get sparkly headbands. Or hair clips."

Suzy's eyes lit up. "If we get all of those things, then I think this dress is perfect."

Aly's smile stretched across her face.

"I agree!" Brooke was touching the flowers. "It's the same color as my sash! We're all going to match so perfectly!"

"I think it's a beautiful choice," Joan said. "And now that you're officially part of the ceremony, that

means you get some responsibilities at the wedding."

"We do?" Suzy and Aly said at the same time.

"You do," Joan affirmed. "I need two people to be in charge of meeting Ralph and his driver and bringing them to the kitchen, where all the leftover food is going to be waiting at the end of the reception. Can you two handle that?"

Aly was nodding before Joan had finished talking. "Absolutely!"

"We can handle that," Suzy said.

Joan tucked Aly's hair behind her ear. "I'm so glad you came up with this solution. I wasn't all that happy about having a wedding without you in it, kiddo."

"And Suzy," Aly added "She came up with the solution too."

"You're right," Joan said. "That was great thinking, Suzy."

"I know. I always have the best ideas," Suzy said.

nine

Inktastic

W e never made our nail polish plan on Saturday. For Joan and Uncle Isaac's wedding."

Without even looking up from her homework, Aly knew who was walking—and, of course, talking—through the Sparkle Spa door. She was expecting customers in the next half hour, but not Suzy this early after school.

"I know, Suzy, I know." Aly had realized that herself right when they'd gotten home from the bridal shop, since she was the one who had to roll the heavy suitcase back inside. "Now that we're junior brides-maids, are we still stylists?" Aly asked.

Suzy shrugged. "I don't see why not."

"Me neither," Brooke said from Sparkly's corner. She was giving him an after-school snack.

Brooke walked over to polish wall. "You know, I was thinking we should make up a special occasion manicure for Joan's wedding."

Suzy rolled her eyes. "Special occasion manicures are—"

"Don't you dare say 'dumb,' Suzy Davis!" Brooke warned.

Aly knew Suzy was absolutely about to say "dumb," and she was glad Brooke had stopped her. "What did you have in mind?" Aly asked her sister.

"Well, I was thinking two colors," Brooke answered. "Heather and I could wear every other finger Pretty in Pink and Turquoise Delight, and you two could wear every other finger Inktastic and Turquoise Delight, so that it matches both of your dresses."

"Sounds pretty," Aly told Brooke. "What about toes?" All four girls would be wearing sandals for the wedding.

"What if I wear turquoise on my toes and you wear black?" Suzy said to Aly.

Aly nodded. "I like it. And Heather can wear pink, and Brooke turquoise."

"Perfect," Brooke said.

Aly grabbed all the color choices from the polish wall. They looked awesome together—all were sparkly, and the pink and turquoise were super bright.

"Joan's going to love this plan," Aly said.

"Uncle Isaac, too," Suzy added.

Aly wasn't so sure that Isaac would really care

about their polish colors, but she kept that opinion to herself.

"Okay," Aly said, "the only thing left is our hair."

Suzy pulled a small stack of papers out of her backpack. It looked like she'd printed them off a computer. "I brought some pictures of sparkly headbands and hair clips. I figured we don't have to match, since Brooke and Heather won't. Plus, our dresses are different colors anyway."

Aly scanned the pages that Suzy spread out on the table in the waiting area. She saw:

- A headband with sparkles all around
- One with a big sparkly flower that matched their sashes
- One with dangly sparkles
- A clip with three sparkly flowers
- Another clip with a sparkly heart

Brooke was peering over Suzy's shoulder. "Sparkles all around is a good choice. Or the sparkle heart clip."

"Not the flowers?" Aly asked.

Brooke shook her head. "You don't want too many flowers," she said. "It's *too* much matching if you have flowers on your waist and in your hair."

"That makes sense," Aly agreed.

Suzy squinted at Brooke. "It actually does."

"So, Suzy, are you thinking headband or clip?"

"Headband," Suzy said.

Aly smiled. "I was thinking clip."

Suzy circled their choices "I'll order them. Now we just have to wait three more weeks to wear them."

Everything was going so well between Aly and Suzy—like they were almost real friends—that it kind of worried Aly. Did that mean something bad was going to happen at the wedding?

ten

I Love Blue, Too

Three weeks later Brooke bounced onto Aly's bed. "It's wedding day!" she sang.

The day before, Aly had polished Brooke's and Suzy's nails. Brooke had polished Aly's and Heather's. All four girls had even taken pictures of their sparkly fingers and toes.

After Aly woke up and Brooke stopped bouncing, the girls headed downstairs for breakfast. In the kitchen Joan, Mom, and Joan's three bridesmaids were sitting at the kitchen table. Michelle was Joan's roommate from college, Julia was her cousin, and Rachel was Isaac's sister, which also made her Suzy Davis's aunt. Mom was giving them each a manicure.

"Want some help?" Aly asked.

"Oh, could you?" Joan answered.

"Of course. Anything for the bride!" Aly said, sticking two pieces of bread in the toaster—one for her and one for Brooke. "What do you need?"

"My toes," Joan said. "Your mom polished them in white yesterday, but then I remembered I needed something blue for good luck. Would you switch it to I Love Blue, Too? Your mom ran to the salon this morning to pick it up for me."

"It's in my purse, Aly," Mom said as she applied a coat of clear polish to Michelle's fingernails.

After eating her toast and putting on latex gloves so the polish remover wouldn't ruin her own manicure,

Aly took off Joan's old polish and repainted her toenails in blue.

"How's that?" Aly asked when she finished.

"I couldn't have done it better myself, kiddo," Joan said.

Aly screwed the cap back on the top coat bottle, then took off her gloves. "I love that I got to do this for you on your wedding day," she told Joan. "And that I get to *be* in your wedding."

"Me too, Aly," Joan said, giving her a hug. "And I love how those alternating-color manicures came out on all you girls."

Aly waved her fingers in the air and smiled. "Thank you," she said.

"You're welcome," Joan answered. "Now go get dressed for my wedding!"

A few hours later the Tanners were on their way to Francie's, one of the nicest restaurants in town that also hosted special events. On the drive over Aly and Brooke didn't move a muscle, not wanting to mess up their nails, hairdos, or new dresses. Dad couldn't believe how beautiful Mom looked and that Brooke was silent for the entire car ride.

When Brooke and Aly walked through the front doors of Francie's, Suzy Davis was there to greet them. "Hurry up, you two. We have to be ready before the other guests arrive." Suzy was going to do their makeup there, and there wasn't a minute to waste.

"You both look fantastic!" Brooke said to Heather and Suzy. "I love the silver eye shadow, Heather."

The girls rushed into the ladies' room, and Suzy quickly worked her makeup magic on the sisters. Aly kept staring at herself in the mirror, hardly recognizing how grown up she looked. Suzy was talented— there was no denying it.

"Thanks, groomsgirl," Aly said with a wink at Suzy.

Fifteen minutes later the bridal party was lined

up, waiting to walk down the aisle. Isaac would be first, followed by Aly and Suzy. The bridesmaids and groomsmen were next in line, with Aly's mom, as matron of honor, and Suzy's dad, as best man, walking together. Jonah, the three-year-old son of one of Isaac's friends, would bring the wedding rings. Next were Brooke and Heather, and then finally, it would be the bride's turn: Joan walking down the aisle with her parents on each side of her.

Aly couldn't believe how nervous she was. "I think I have to pee," she whispered to Suzy.

"You do not have to pee," Suzy whispered back. "You just peed ninety seconds ago."

It was true; Aly had just gotten back from the bathroom.

"You're just nervous," Suzy continued. "It's going to be fine. Stop worrying."

Aly tried to stop worrying, but there were so many

people there and her dress was so long. What if she tripped? Aly took a deep breath.

"Seriously," Suzy said, "whatever it is you're worried about probably won't happen."

"I'm worried I'll trip," Aly told her.

"Want to know a trick my mom taught me about that?" Suzy said.

Aly nodded. Why didn't *her* mom teach her a trick?

"You hold your skirt a little off the floor, like this." Suzy demonstrated by pinching just a little part of her skirt, right where her hand fell against her leg, and lifting it a tiny bit. "Now you won't trip."

Aly tried it, and it made her feel much calmer. Then the music started.

Suzy tugged Aly's arm, and they were walking down the aisle. Every guest was taking pictures. Aly was smiling her biggest smile and admiring all of the flowers strung along the sides of the chairs. She felt herself wobble a little, but she held tightly to Suzy.

"Nice job not falling," Suzy hissed through her smile.

After what seemed like the longest walk of Aly's life, the girls finally got to the front of the aisle. Aly forked to the left, Suzy to the right, and each stood on opposite sides of the judge, where they watched the rest of the wedding party come down the aisle.

Everyone laughed when Brooke started waving as she and Heather walked together. *My sister doesn't have a nervous bone in her body,* Aly thought.

An old Beatles song started playing. Joan appeared. Aly knew it was Joan, but she didn't look anything like the manicurist and baker Aly saw every day. She looked completely transformed. Her dress was a princess-style ball gown covered in beads and lace. A long veil flowed behind her as she walked. Or floated, it seemed.

"Oooh," everyone said, including Aly.

Joan and Isaac looked at each other like they were the only two people in the room. Brooke sent Aly a Secret Sister Message: *Isn't this amazing?* Aly started to send one back, but she couldn't . . . she had started crying. She gazed out at the guests and realized she wasn't alone: It looked like everyone was crying happy tears.

Aly glanced over at Suzy. Even she had tears on her cheeks, and Aly wasn't surprised one little bit.

eleven

Good Knight

After the ceremony there was a cocktail hour, followed by dinner and dancing. Brooke and Aly made sure to dance to every single song they possibly could, including the last one—another old Beatles tune during which they danced with their mom and dad, all as a group, sort of like a big, swaying hug.

Halfway through, Dad turned and kissed Mom.

"Ew," Brooke said.

But Aly thought it was nice that her parents liked to kiss each other.

At the end of the song the best man started tapping a water glass with a spoon. Other guests joined in, and then Isaac leaned over and kissed Joan.

"Double ew," Brooke said.

Mom put her arm around Brooke's shoulders. "One day soon I bet you won't think it's quite so gross. Right, Al?"

Aly smiled. She liked being counted as a grown-up.

A grown-up! That made Aly remember that she and Suzy were in charge of helping Ralph with the food donation.

"I've got to go prep for Rock & Wrap It Up," she said hurriedly. "See you later." Then she took off to find Suzy.

The two girls waited outside Francie's until the truck arrived. They led Ralph and his driver, Ari, back to the kitchen.

"Do you need some help carrying the food?" Aly

asked when she saw all the trays, boxes, and bags lining the counter.

"Actually," Ralph said, "that would be great."

"Aly," Suzy hissed. "We'll ruin our dresses."

But Aly ignored her. She picked up a box full of crackers and a bag full of rolls. "Come on, Suzy," she said.

Suzy huffed, but then she hoisted a crate of broccoli and followed Ralph to the truck. "I can't believe I'm spending my uncle's wedding carrying broccoli to a truck," she grumbled.

"Stop it," Aly said. "The wedding is basically over, and this will only take five minutes. Besides, I think it's pretty awesome that Isaac and Joan are doing this. So many people who might not have enough food to eat are going to get a lot now."

"I guess you're right," Suzy said. "That is pretty cool."

"And it's cool that we got to be junior brides-maids," Aly added. "And groomsgirls."

Suzy slid the crate she was carrying onto the truck. "And that we got to do this together."

Aly looked at Suzy, narrowing her eyes. "Have we become friends?" she asked.

At the beginning of the school year—or even two months ago—Aly never would have believed that she could be friends with mean Suzy Davis. But now, even though Suzy was still kind of prickly and spoke her mind all the time, Aly had grown to appreciate her. She appreciated her ideas and the way she kept at something until she was happy with the way it turned out. And it also turned out that she and Suzy weren't a bad team.

"I think we have," Suzy answered, helping Aly stuff her load into the truck.

"Hmm," Aly said. "I think I like that."

"I think I do too," Suzy said. She gave Aly a high five.

Just then Isaac called out, "Don't move!" He pulled a small digital camera from his pocket and snapped their picture. "That's a great image to include in our wedding album." He showed them the photo of their nail polish shimmering against the Good Knight–colored sky.

"You know what I realized, Aly?" he said. "This day never would have happened if it weren't for the Sparkle Spa. It wasn't until I came in to take pictures for Paws for Love's Adoption Day that I realized how special Joan was. So, really, I have you and the Sparkle Spa to thank for this wedding."

Aly smiled. It turned out the Sparkle Spa was even more awesome than she and Brooke had ever imagined it could be.

How to Give Yourself (or a Friend!) a Wedding Bells Pedicure
By Aly (and Brooke!)

* . + * . + * . + . + * . + * . + *

What you need:

Paper towels

Polish remover

Cotton balls

   (Or you can just use more paper towels.)

Clear polish

Two colorful polishes

   (Any two colors will work fine, but we
   like it best when the colors are very
   different, like pink and turquoise or purple
   and yellow.)

What you do:

1. Place some paper towels on the floor—or wherever you're going to put your feet—so you don't have to worry if the nail polish doesn't do a good job of going where you mean for it to go. (The only exception to this rule is if you're polishing your toes outside on the grass. But even then someone might get mad if the grass turns colors.)

2. Take a cotton ball or a folded-up paper towel and put some polish remover on it. If you have polish on your toes already, use enough to get it off. If you don't, just rub the remover over your nails once to get off any dirt that might be on there. (Because dirt is . . . dirty!) Also, the nail polish stays better when you do this before polishing. (We have no idea why.)

3. Rip off two more paper towels. Roll the first one into a tube and twist it so it stays that way. Then weave it back and forth between your toes to separate them a little bit more. After that, do the same thing with the second paper towel for your other foot. You might need to tuck it in around your pinkie toe if it pops up and gets in your way while you polish—you can also cut the paper towel to make it shorter if you want. (Aly doesn't like ripping it, because sometimes too much gets ripped, but I think it's fine to do that.)

4. Open up your clear polish and paint a coat on each nail. Then close the bottle up tight. (You can do any order, but Aly usually starts with my big toes and works her way to my pinkies.)

5. Open up the first colored polish. Use it to polish the big toe, middle toe, and pinkie toe on your left foot. Then use it to polish the second and fourth toes on your right foot. Put the cap back on tight. (Tight is important, just in case your polish tips over.)

6. Open up the second colored polish. Use it to polish the big toe, middle toe, and pinkie toe on your right foot. Then use it to polish the second and fourth toes on your left foot. (Basically, just polish the toes with no polish on them! Aly makes it so complicated.) Put the cap back on tight.

7. Repeat step five.

8. Repeat step six.

9. Blow on your toes or just let them dry for, like, a minute. Then open up your clear polish. Do a top coat of clear polish on all your toes. Close the bottle up tight. (Remember: tight!)

10. Your toes have to dry. You can fan them for a long time, or sit and make a bracelet or read a book or watch TV or talk to your friend (or sister!) until you're all dry. Usually it takes about twenty minutes, but it could take longer. (Which is why we try to find fun things to do while our nails dry. Otherwise, sitting in one place for twenty minutes is bor-ing.)

Now you should have a beautiful wedding bells pedicure! Even after the polish is dry, you proba-bly shouldn't wear socks and sneaker-type shoes for a while. Bare feet or sandals are better so all your hard work doesn't get smooshed. (And so you can show off your two-toned toes!)

Happy polishing!

＊ ． ＊ ． ＊ ． ＊ ． ＊ ． ＊

For more Sparkle Spa fun including polls, nail designs, and more visit SparkleSpaBooks.com!